The Pirates of Bat Cave Island

A Treasure-Hunting Flap Book

By Burton Albert
Illustrations by Margeaux Lucas

Little
Simon

The ship sailed toward the tiny island.
Wind flapped the black flag on top of
the mainmast. It showed a skull and crossbones.
Soon the ship landed. Over its sides
tumbled . . .

They had come to find a treasure.
They had seen clues about it on a map
they had robbed—days earlier—from
another boat of buccaneers, the S.S.
Plunderwell.

The wild crew ran to shore. Their daggers
glinted in the sun. As Captain Mole-Nose
cut through the sky-high grass, he saw . . .

They were secret signs! And they looked exactly like those on the piece of parchment from the *Plunderwell*. The first sign meant "Go 'round the big trees."

The captain unfolded the map and checked for the other sign. Sure enough! It was below the drawing of . . .

Petunia, the captain's pet parrot, flew from Mole-Nose's shoulder to his wrist. She flapped her yellow-green wings excitedly. Under her wing, the ship's master rubbed . . .

He wished for good luck.

"Look for more signs!" the captain howled.

His merry band clomped further on. But lo and behold, Red-Eye Rufus didn't watch where he was walking. And what at first looked like a mound of moss and mushrooms turned out to be . . .

"EEEOWW!" the pirates screamed, and dashed in a flash—through the fields of grass.

Soon they saw other markings. One looked like this: . It, too, was on the map. It meant "Go on ahead."

But in the foggy mist the pirates could hardly figure out anything in front of them. Not until they nearly bumped into it did they see . . .

It had a door for a mouth. Tattoo Tessie tugged at the ring of a handle. As the door gave out a rusty, squeaky *crrreeak*, she and her mates suddenly fell into a pit. Their arms and legs flew all about.

Above them the open doorway led only to more woods and sky. It was, indeed, part of a trap to keep them from finding the treasure.

On the wall of the rock Captain Mole-Nose noticed two other signs. The sign  meant "Cross the water."

The other, , meant "Look for caves." The desperate pirates tried to climb the walls of the pit, but the rock was too slippery.

An idea whizzed into the captain's mind.

"Sackbottom! Blue Boots! Make a ladder of vines!" Then the pirates scrambled up the knotted stems and headed for the murmur of water. Watching them among a twist of branches sat . . .

And in a nearby swamp, hidden by the brown tips of cattails, floated a pile of . . .

Night fell as the pirates swam across the river. Soon after, from behind the dark clouds of a full moon, flew . . .

All were coming from the same place. "Over there!" the captain bellowed. "It's the hidden cave!"

The pirates ran toward the opening. They cast strange, wiggly shadows on the ground, especially when their lanterns caught on tangles of . . .

As they entered the cave, the pirates squinted into blackness. Staring back at them were a thousand pairs of eyes.

"Yikes! Ghosts!" shrieked Two-Tooth, the ship's cooper. And he hopped upon Sack's back, holding on to it tighter than one of the barrels he had made on deck. But as lanterns lit up the walls, Two-Tooth gave a big sigh. The eyes were nothing more than those of . . .

On the dirt floor lay some pebbles. They were shaped like this: ☠ .

"It must be another sign," he said. The captain pored over his map. "Yes! It must mean 'Dig. The treasure is under here!'" And with their daggers the pirates dug like dogs after a bone.

A few feet down they heard a clunk. "It's the chest! Scoop out around it," the captain whispered. He wanted no one but his crew to hear.

The chest was covered with a stack of bones. Quickly the pirates scraped away the gritty soil and found the face of . . .

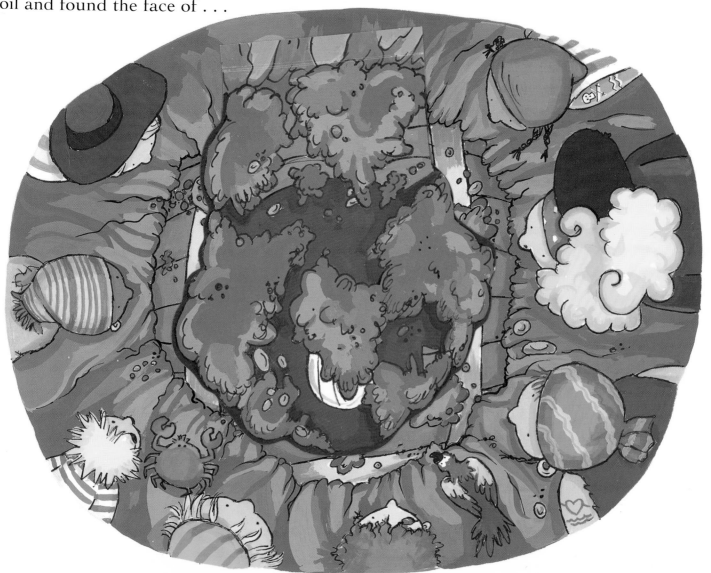

It had been painted there to scare away ghosts.

Slowly the pirates opened the buried chest. Their eyes popped! Inside was a skull. They at last found themselves staring at something they would never, *ever* forget. The skeleton's mouth, in a devilish grin, was filled with . . .